T0338397

Thank You Day

adapted by Farrah McDoogle

based on the screenplay "Neighborhood Thank You Day"

written by Angela C. Santomero and Becky Friedman

poses and layouts by Gord Garwood

Ready-to-Read

Simon Spotlight

New York   London   Toronto   Sydney   New Delhi

SIMON SPOTLIGHT
An imprint of Simon & Schuster Children's Publishing Division
1230 Avenue of the Americas, New York, New York 10020
© 2014 The Fred Rogers Company
SIMON SPOTLIGHT, READY-TO-READ, and colophon are registered trademarks of Simon & Schuster, Inc.
For information about special discounts for bulk purchases, please contact
Simon & Schuster Special Sales at 1-866-506-1949 or business@simonandschuster.com.
The Simon & Schuster Speakers Bureau can bring authors to your live event. For more information or to
book an event contact the Simon & Schuster Speakers Bureau at 1-866-248-3049 or visit our
website at www.simonspeakers.com.
Manufactured in the United States of America 0823 LAK
6 8 10 9 7
ISBN 978-1-4424-9833-4 (pbk)
ISBN 978-1-4424-9834-1 (hc)
ISBN 978-1-4424-9835-8 (eBook)

Today we say thank you to all the people we love.

We say thank you
to show them we care.

That is the Thank You tree.

We hang thank you notes

in the tree!

Today I will write a note and put it on the tree!

The wind blew a note off the tree!

My grandpa catches
the note.
What does it say?

The note is from
my grandpa to me!
What do the other notes say?

Katerina says thank you
to her mommy!

Prince Wednesday says
thank you to his brother.

"Thank you for playing ball with me!"

Teacher Harriet will put the thank you notes on the tree!

Who should I say thank you to?

Now I know who to say thank you to!

Thank you, Mr. McFeely!
"You are welcome!" says
Mr. McFeely.